D0471137

KEEPING A CHRISTMAS SECRET

TOYS

KEEPING A CHRISTMAS SECRET

by Phyllis Reynolds Naylor

illustrated by Lena Shiffman

Atheneum 1989 New York

Books for Younger Readers by Phyllis Reynolds Naylor

How Lazy Can You Get?
All Because I'm Older
The Boy with the Helium Head
Old Sadie and the Christmas Bear
Keeping a Christmas Secret

Text copyright © 1989 by Phyllis Reynolds Naylor
Illustrations copyright © 1989 by Lena Shiffman

All rights reserved. No part of this book may be reproduced or transmitted in any form or by any means, electronic or mechanical, including photocopying, recording, or by any information storage and retrieval system, without permission in writing from the publisher.

Atheneum
Macmillan Publishing Company
866 Third Avenue, New York, NY 10022
Collier Macmillan Canada, Inc.
First Edition
Printed in Singapore

10 9 8 7 6 5 4 3 2 1

Library of Congress Cataloging-in-Publication Data
Naylor, Phyllis Reynolds.
Keeping a Christmas secret/by Phyllis Reynolds Naylor : illustrated by Lena Shiffman. p. cm.
Summary: Four-year-old Michael finds a way to redeem himself after he mistakenly tells Dad what the family is giving him for Christmas.
ISBN 0-689-31447-7
[1. Secrets—Fiction. 2. Gifts—Fiction. 3. Christmas—Fiction.]
I. Shiffman, Lena, ill. II. Title.
PZ7.N24Ch 1989 [E]—dc19 88-29277 CIP AC

To Michael, who knows why

—P. R. N.

For Brian, for all his love and support

—L. S.

It was two days before Christmas. Michael and his family were shopping for a present for Dad. There, in the store window, was a blue-and-silver sled with sturdy runners that shone like scissors.

"Wait!" said Michael, who was only four. "That would make a good present!"

"Dad would be so surprised!" Betsy said.

"Yes, he would," agreed Mother. "Let's buy it."

So they did and took it home.

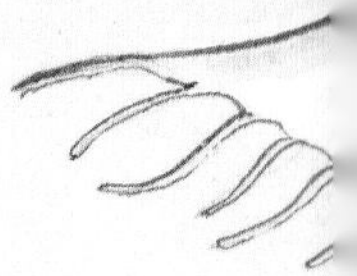

"Don't *tell*, now," Tim warned Michael as they carried the sled into the kitchen.

"I won't," Michael promised.

“Don’t *tell*!” Betsy reminded him later, as they wrapped the sled in bright red paper.

“I won’t,” Michael said. “*I* can keep a secret!”

"Well," said Dad that evening, when they all sat down to dinner, "what did my family do today?"

"Went shopping," said Michael.

"Shhh!" said Tim and Betsy.

"Did you get a present for me?" Father asked, smiling.

"Don't *tell*!" Betsy said to Michael.

"Aha!" said Father, teasing. "Does it have wheels? I've always wanted a new car."

"No," said Tim, laughing.

"Does it have a sail?" Father went on. "I've always wanted a boat."

"No," said Betsy, giggling.

"Does it have a whistle?" Father asked. "I've always wanted a train."

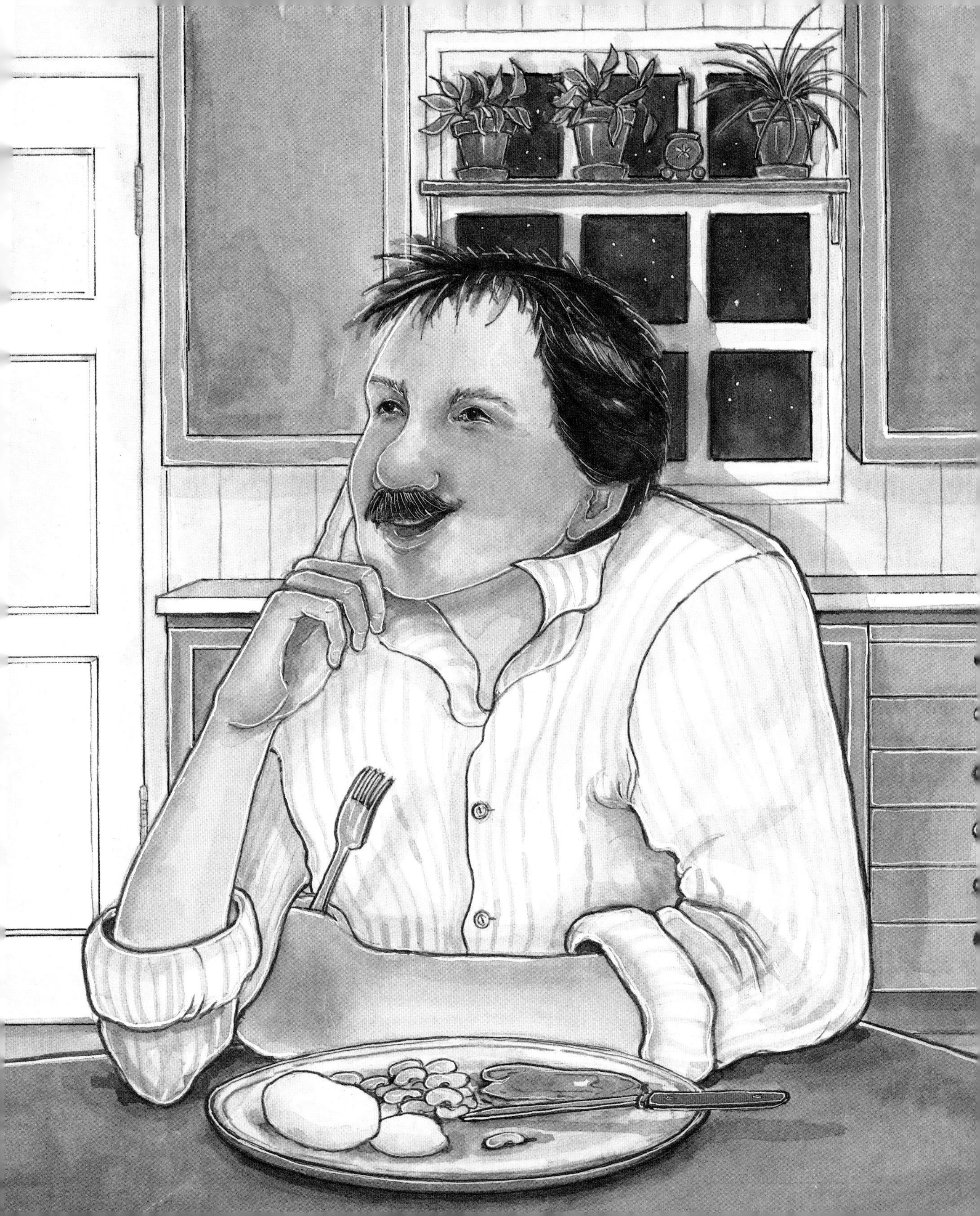

"No!" said Michael. "It has runners."

"Michael!" yelled Tim and Betsy together.

"I didn't tell!" Michael cried. "I didn't say it was a sled!"

"Oh, Michael!" said Mother.

"You're a jerk, Michael," Betsy told him.

"You ruined our surprise for Dad," said Tim.

"It's my fault," Dad said. "I shouldn't have asked so many questions."

Michael couldn't believe he had told the secret.

"Big deal!" Tim would say when Father opened the package on Christmas morning, because it wouldn't be a surprise now at all.

Michael wasn't hungry anymore. He ate one bite of his pork chop, three lima beans, and a corner off his chocolate brownie. Then he got down from the table.

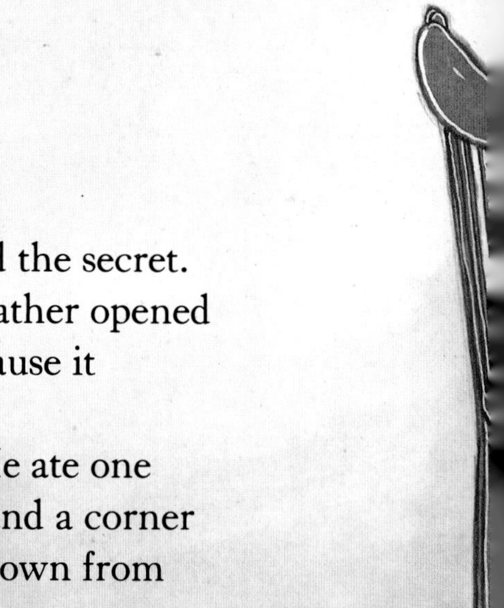

While Tim and Betsy were watching television, however, Michael got an idea. He thought of something that no one else in the family had thought about. Not yet, anyway.

Michael poked through his toys until he found what he was looking for. Then he stuffed it into an empty spaghetti box.

He cut out pictures of snowmen from a catalogue and taped them over the words on the box.

"What are you doing, Michael?" Betsy asked.

"I'm not telling," said Michael.

"What's in the box?" Tim wanted to know.

"It's a secret," Michael said.

When he had finished, Michael put the present under the sled beneath the tree. Everyone turned to look.

"And I *won't* tell!" Michael said.

On Christmas morning, when all the other gifts had been opened, Father unwrapped the sled.

"Some surprise!" said Betsy glumly.

"I didn't know it was going to be blue and silver!" Dad said. "Those are my favorite colors."

"Big deal!" muttered Tim.

"In fact," said Dad, "I'd like to go sledding right now."

"Right *now*?" asked Michael.

"This very minute," said Dad.

Then he saw the spaghetti box. "What's this?" he asked.

"I don't know," said Mother.

"Nobody knows but Michael," Betsy told them.

"It's a secret," said Michael. "And you can't open it unless you guess what's inside."

"A Hershey bar," guessed Tim.

"Pencils," said Betsy.

Michael shook his head.

"Spaghetti?" asked Mother.

"A green necktie with pink and purple polka dots," said Father.

Michael laughed and hid the box behind his back. "You didn't guess," he told them. "Now you'll have to wait."

They put on their coats and caps and boots, and Father drove them to the top of the hill behind the school. Everyone piled on the sled together, and soon they were racing down toward the trees below.

Snowflakes blew against their faces. Other families watched and waved. When the sled stopped, they all rolled off, laughing.

“Oh, no!” said Mother, as they brushed themselves off. “Do you know what we don’t have? A rope to pull the sled.”

Father groaned. “Don’t tell me I have to drive all the way home again to get one.”

“We could take turns carrying the sled back up the hill,” Mother suggested.

“It’s too big!” Tim whined.

“It’s too heavy!” said Betsy. “I can’t do it.”

“Well, I’m not going to carry it if Betsy’s not,” said Tim.

“We’re not going to ruin Christmas by quarreling, are we?” asked Mother.

“Surprise!” yelled Michael, as he pulled the spaghetti box out from under his jacket.

Tim and Betsy stared while Father opened the box. Inside was an old jump rope with the handles missing.

"Yea!" yelled Tim. "A rope for the sled! We won't have to carry it after all."

"And I don't have to drive back home to get a rope," said Father.

"Thank goodness!" said Mother. "And we won't have to listen to any more quarreling."

"So *that* was the secret you were working on," said Tim, as they tied the rope to the sled. "Nice going, Mike!"

"And this time you didn't tell!" said Betsy.

Up the hill they went, Mother and Betsy first, then Tim, then Father, and finally Michael, pulling the blue-and-silver sled, all the way to the top.